The Heart of a Friendship

Dear Mackenzie,
Enjoy reading and
telling favorite
stories with
you loving family
and friends
too!

Heather St

The Heart of a Friendship

An East African Folktale

**Retold by
H. J. Arrington**

**Illustrated by
JoAnn E. Kitchel**

PELICAN PUBLISHING COMPANY
Gretna 1997

*To my son, Jaime, who is my inspiration and my greatest fan, and
to my mother, for always believing in me*

*The word "Pelican" and the depiction of a pelican are trademarks
of Pelican Publishing Company, Inc., and are registered
in the U.S. Patent and Trademark Office.*

Library of Congress Cataloguing-in-Publication Data

Arrington, H. J.
 The heart of a friendship : an East African folktale / retold by
H.J. Arrington ; illustrated by JoAnn E. Kitchel.
  p.   cm.
 Summary: In this East African folktale, the friendship between a mango-
eating monkey and a crocodile is tested when the leader of all crocodiles falls
ill and needs to eat a monkey's heart to be cured.
 ISBN 1-56554-224-X (alk. paper)
 [1. Folklore—Africa, East.] I. Kitchel, JoAnn E., ill.
II. Title.
PZ8.1.A76He 1997
398.2'09676'045—dc20
[E]   96-42238
                                                                        CIP
                                                                        AC

Printed in Hong Kong

Published by Pelican Publishing Company, Inc.
1101 Monroe Street, Gretna, Louisiana 70053

THE HEART OF A FRIENDSHIP

Long, long ago, near the coast of Kenya,
there lived a monkey named Taki. Taki lived
high up in the branches of a great mango tree.
From his home, he could look out far and wide
over the great winding river.

On the branches of the mango tree grew the mango fruit. This fruit was tasty and delicious; it provided much nourishment to Taki. Every day, Taki would sit on the branches that hung out over the water and eat his juicy and delicious fruit. Sometimes, the only sound you could hear was Taki happily munching his fruit. Yum, yum, yum. Yum, yum, yum.

Now it so happened that a crocodile named Baku lived at the other end of the river. One day when he was out exploring, he noticed the little monkey feasting. For many days, Baku swam by and watched the hungry little monkey eating the fruit. It looked so good! Baku just had to have some.

One day he swam close to the shore and shouted at Taki, "Hey! Hey you up there! Throw down a piece of that fruit. You've got plenty and I'm very hungry."

"Are you talking to me?" Taki asked quietly.

"Of course I am. Come on, please give me just one piece."

"Don't call me 'Hey you.' My name is Taki. And whom, may I ask, are you?" Taki said as he stretched to get a better look at his visitor.

"I am Baku, the crocodile. I didn't mean to be rude. It's just that every day when I come this way, I see you enjoying that fruit. I am hungry. And it looks sooo good."

Taki replied, "It is good. It tastes like nothing else." Taki looked down at Baku. Then he tossed a large fruit to the crocodile.

Quick as lightning, Baku snapped up the fruit in his huge jaws. Chomp, chomp, chomp. "Ohhh, Taki. A taste so wonderful! Thank you for sharing."

Taki smiled. "So, you do have some manners. I'm glad you enjoyed it."

The next day, Baku came back. Taki shared his fruit with the crocodile again. And so it was. Every day, Baku would come to visit Taki and they would eat the juicy, delicious fruit. Yum, yum, yum. Chomp, chomp, chomp. This is how their friendship began. Taki would toss fruit to Baku. The two would eat and talk. Talk and eat. The days turned into weeks. Taki and Baku became good friends.

But one day, when Baku came to visit, he shouted up to Taki, "Wait, my friend. Don't toss me any fruit. I would like to invite you to come to my house for dinner."

"Oh Baku, how nice. But I can't go in the water. I cannot swim and I would certainly drown."

"I would not let that happen. I want you to ride on my back. You will be safe that way."

Taki quickly skittered down the great fruit tree. Baku swam close to the sandy shore. Taki jumped upon Baku's back and held on tightly. Off they went, out into the warm blue waters.

When they had gone a little way, far enough that Taki could not get back to shore, Baku began to speak. "Taki. I have something to tell you. It is something I do not wish to say."

"What is it? Tell me, my friend," Taki said quietly.

"I have tricked you. We are not going to dinner. But it is all my fault. I should never have boasted of our friendship. I . . . " Baku's words rushed out of his mouth.

"Slow down, Baku. I do not understand."
"They made me come and get you. I told them about the fruit and about our friendship. Our Mighty One is so ill, we have no choice," Baku said quickly.

In a firm voice, Taki said, "What do you mean? Do you need some of my delicious fruit? Tell me clearly. What is it?"

"The Mighty One, the leader of all crocodiles, is gravely ill.
The council of the wise agrees that the only thing that will cure
him is to eat a piece of loyalty. And it is written that one can
find it . . . in a . . . a monkey's heart. So I was sent to get you."
Baku was finally quiet.

Taki's breath caught in his throat. "My heart? My heart? I
cannot believe this!"

Baku said, "I didn't want to do it. They made me come. Oh, I
should never have boasted so of our friendship!"

Taki was silent, but just for a moment. Luckily, he was a quick-thinking monkey. He said, "Of course I will help. We must save your Mighty One."

"You will? We must? Uhh, I mean, of course we must! Yes, yes!"

"But, Baku. You should have told me earlier. You don't know about monkeys, do you? But then, how would you know? You see, monkeys never, ever take their hearts away from home. My heart is back in the great mango tree, high up in the branches. And it is full of loyalty!"

"It is?" Baku said in surprise.

"Yes, yes. But hurry, Baku. Turn around quickly. Take me back and I'll get it for you. Hurry! We don't have a minute to lose! Your leader is dying!"

Baku turned around as quickly as he could. He swam like the wind, carrying Taki back to the shore beneath the great mango tree. Before he could even get close enough for a safe jump, Taki splashed into the water and bounded to the shore. Then he quickly skittered up the fruit tree. Taki disappeared from sight in the large, high branches.

All was quiet. After several minutes had passed, Baku yelled up to Taki. "Taki, hurry up!"

Only silence greeted Baku's ears.

The crocodile waited. He started to get angry. "Taki! Can't you find your heart? Is your house that cluttered?"

There was no answer from Taki.

Now Baku was beginning to get nervous. He began to sweat (and that's pretty hard for a crocodile to do). "Taki," Baku whined. "Taki, what is wrong? Can't you hear me?" In a louder voice, he shouted, "Taki, bring me your heart!"

At last, from the very top of the tree, came Taki's reply. In a firm yet quiet voice, he said, "You foolish beast. You had loyalty in your hands more than once but lost it each time. Go back and face your people empty-handed. There is no loyalty in your heart, so you do not deserve mine."

And that's the end of that.